# THE MAGIC SKATEBOARD

# THE MAGIC SKATEBOARD

# Enid Richemont

Illustrations by Jan Ormerod

## CANDLEWICK PRESS
CAMBRIDGE, MASSACHUSETTS

Text copyright © 1991 by Enid Richemont
Illustrations copyright © 1991 by Jan Ormerod

First U.S. edition 1992
First published in Great Britain in 1991 by
Walker Books Ltd., London.

*Library of Congress Cataloging-in-Publication Data:*

Richemont, Enid.   The magic skateboard/Enid Richemont :
illustrations by Jan Ormerod. — 1st U.S. ed.
Summary: On his way home from school in London just before
Chistmas, Danny meets a strange-looking woman who
transforms his skateboard into a kind of flying carpet that
allows him to visit any place he imagines.
[1. Magic—Fiction. 2. Skateboards—Fiction. 3. Blacks—
England—Fiction. 4. London (England)—Fiction.]
I. Ormerod, Jan, ill.   II. Title.
PZ7. R39839Mag   1993   [Fic]—dc20   92-53010
ISBN 1-56402-132-7

10 9 8 7 6 5 4 3 2 1

Printed in the U.S.A.

Candlewick Press
2067 Massachusetts Avenue
Cambridge, Massachusetts 02140

For Danny

# Chapter One

It was exactly five days before Christmas.

It was a day when you could do anything.

They'd brought in cookies and potato chips and popped open cans of soda.

They'd painted their faces and put on a show.

They'd yelled, "See you next year!" to Mr. O'Sullivan.

At four o'clock it was already dusk. The first star glimmered through the soccer netting, and the glow from the streetlights brushed silver over leaves as brittle as ribbon candy.

The last teacher to leave called out, "Watch it, you guys! You'll be locked in!"

Danny and his gang, puffing like dragons, squeaked open the school gate and stood huddled on the sidewalk.

Usually they would have hung around until five or even later, for they all lived close by. But it was cold. Too cold for snow even, people were saying, and too chilly to fool around in the street when every lit window was making them think of warmth and food and television.

So they broke up.

"See ya."

"Bye."

Danny had lost his gloves, and his fingers ached with the cold. He put down his skateboard and scraped slowly along the frost-powdered sidewalk, thinking of supper and Christmas, and Christmas and supper.

He didn't hear the lady coming. He didn't see her until his face hit something soft and squishy, and his nose was tickled by a feathery thing that smelled of cinnamon and mothballs.

"Sorry," he said. It was always happening, he thought, and it wasn't fair. *He* had to balance. All they had to do was walk.

He sneezed.

"Bless you."

Danny looked up at her.

Up and up . . .

And up.

For she was the tallest woman Danny had ever seen, and certainly the strangest. Her ragged velvet coat was the color of ripe plums, and an inch or two of tattered silk skirt drooped over boots as glossy as a beetle's back. Her scarf of black ostrich feathers brushed the ground, and a black straw hat trimmed with violets was tied under her chin with black netting. Her hair — the little he could see of it — was white, and her face was as wrinkled as a prune, but her eyes were bright and wickedly alert.

Danny stared at her. He just couldn't help it.

"That is an interesting toy you have," she said at last. "A . . . skateboard, I believe it is called."

Her voice was clear and strong, but she said her words a little too carefully, as if she had just learned them from a book.

Silly old woman, thought Danny; a skateboard isn't a toy.

He nodded. "That's right."

"May I look at it?"

No, you can't, he thought irritably, handing it over.

He saw her long, black-gloved fingers moving over the board, stroking its surface, touching its curved edges, as if she had never seen anything like it.

Danny watched her in amazement. Lots of people had skateboards. Where had she come from?

She was probably crazy.

She was probably nuts.

And old. Even older than his grandma.

She started playing with the rollers. They seemed to fascinate her. With a flick of her fingers, she set them spinning. The spinning seemed to please her, and she did it again. And again. And again.

Just like my kid brother, thought Danny scornfully. Just like some itsy-bitsy baby.

Then she smiled — the small, satisfied smile people give when they've just finished making something.

"Thank you." She handed it back to him.

Danny tucked it under his arm. He wriggled uncomfortably, feeling her watching him, her eyes twinkling, her face crinkling, as if they were sharing some special secret.

"Are you," she said, "very skillful at this . . . skateboarding?"

Danny shrugged.

He was working at it, wasn't he?

Anyway, what did she know?

"Watch this," he said, crossing his fingers.

He put down the board and skated a short distance along the street. Concentrating hard, he performed a shaky kick-turn, flapping his arms to balance. Then he came right back at her, swerving aside only at the last minute.

Scared you! Scared you! he thought gleefully, hoping she'd squeal and jump, the way his sister always did.

But she just went on standing there. Looking at him.

Danny picked up his board.

He was cold.

He was hungry.

And anyway, his mom didn't like him talking to strangers.

# Chapter Two

"Wait!"

The woman's voice was unexpectedly bossy.

Danny hesitated.

She smiled.

"May I try?" she asked politely.

He blinked. She had to be joking.

But she slid the skateboard out from under his arm and set it on the ground.

Danny watched, speechless.

Well, what was there to say?

Weird, he thought. A real nutcase.

She kicked off. He held his breath.

"You'll fall," he shouted, but somehow he knew that her balance would be perfect.

And it was.

She skated to the end of the street, a ridiculous figure, her long skirts flapping in the breeze, and the feather scarf curling around her like a flying caterpillar. She turned and came back.

"I shall try some turns now," she said.

"Oh, no!" protested Danny. "I mean, you need to be good to do turns. I mean, you need to practice. And you have to have knee pads . . ."

The woman ignored him.

Delicately she placed one black boot on the skateboard.

"Is this how you start?"

She pushed off sideways. She closed her eyes and began to spin. Faster and faster. The board was moving so quickly now that Danny could no longer make out its shape.

The coat and the ragged skirt whirled into a plum-colored spinning top. Her face spun like white cotton candy, but her eyes kept watching him, like shiny black grapes, dark and wicked, teasing him.

She slowed down and stopped.

"I did not fall," she said smugly.

Danny drew a breath. "Can I have it back now?" he asked in a small voice.

"Be patient."

She began to fool around with the skateboard, rocking it from side to side across the sidewalk.

Danny was worried. It *had* been his birthday present.

"Okay, so you're good," he muttered.

She began to bounce it against someone's front yard wall.

"Oh, stop it!" he shouted.

She began to slide up the wall. Up and up. She slid over the neat privet hedge — he could hear the rollers scraping over frozen leaves.

For a second she disappeared. Then he saw her. She was skateboarding up the front of the house, carefully avoiding the windows. In one of those windows, a girl, her back to the street, was wrapping a paper streamer around the bars of her bunk bed. Danny gaped in disbelief. That girl had seen nothing, knew nothing.

"Danny!"

He looked up, and there was the woman, sitting astride the roof, laughing, waving. In one hand she held his skateboard.

"Catch!" she shouted.

"Oh, no!" yelled Danny, but his hands shot out and the skateboard fell into them as gently as a beach ball.

"It's yours," she said.

"I know," said Danny.

"But it is also mine."

Danny's watch began to beep. Irritated, he switched it off. Then he noticed the time. Four-thirty? But he'd set it to go off at five . . .

High above his head, the woman was chuckling.

"My Time," she said. "I will share it with you. Until your watch speaks again, do with your skateboard whatever you wish . . ." She pulled a green-and-red sparkler out of the sky. "Merry Christmas, Danny," she called.

She did a backward somersault into the air.
For one moment she hung, suspended between
rooftop and sky. Then, stretching out an arm
like a swimmer, she began to glide in a great
curve, over the street, over the school at the end
of the street, and away.

Danny watched, open-mouthed, running,
moving to follow the path of her flight. He
watched until the flapping skirts and the pale
face became nothing but a violet rag blown by

the wind. He watched until they turned into a thin line drawn with a purple crayon, and he watched that line until it winked out of sight somewhere over the park. Even then he went on looking, half expecting her to reappear, listening for her mocking laughter.

After a while, his neck began to ache. He shook himself and looked around.

It was the same old street. Nothing had changed. There were the frozen sycamores with their dappled trunks. There was the streetlight someone had smashed. There were the swear words sprayed on the wall, and there, at the end of the street, rose the dark, familiar shape of his school. The same old cars were parked along the road — the red station wagon and the dirty van with WASH ME finger-painted in dust.

Pop music suddenly blared from an open door. A cat howled.

Danny shivered.

She fooled me, he thought. It had all been a trick. And anyway, I'm hungry.

# Chapter Three

Danny looked at his skateboard.

It was the same skateboard. A good one, but ordinary. Nothing special about it, apart from the fact that months ago, his dad had given it to him for his birthday.

He thought again about those stunts the old lady had pulled off. It had to be a trick. You just couldn't do things like that on a skateboard. Even if you were good. Even if you were a champ. Nobody could.

He wondered if she'd fiddled with it in some way, damaged it, messed it up. Worried, he put it down on the sidewalk. He stepped on it, trying it out, rocking it gently from side to side. She had skateboarded over the hedge — now *that* was impossible. And up the front of the house.

How did it feel, he wondered, to skateboard up the front of a house?

Suddenly, he knew. Up and over the hedge he went.

He should have fallen off.

He did not.

He should have been terrified.

He was not.

Below him, the yards
and the street moved
rapidly away as
Danny carefully
avoided the
windows. And
up the slope of
the roof he went
until he stood
at the
very top.

He wasn't scared. He knew he wouldn't fall. He didn't know how he knew. He just knew.

He was a bird. He was a golden eagle. He was Superman. He could do anything on that skateboard. Anything at all.

My Time, she'd said. We share it. Do with it whatever you wish.

Now he understood. Whatever you wish, she had said. Whatever you wish.

He took a deep breath and thought of the sidewalk. It worked! In one smooth movement he was down. This was fantastic! He thought of the rooftop, and once again he stood with his head in the sky. Down he went again, laughing out loud. Up and down. Up and down.

Who was the greatest?

Danny was the greatest!

He longed to show someone. He wanted to shock passers by, but there were no passers by. He wanted to show off to his friends, but they had long since gone home. He thought about his mom, who always said she was unshockable. He thought about his older sister, who teased him, and his little brother, who pestered him.

And instantly he was in his own front yard. A

cat sprang into the air, hissed, and vanished through a hole in the hedge. He giggled. Wait till his mom saw him skating up the roof.

He was going to ring the doorbell, when he paused. Until your watch speaks again, she'd said; it might do that right now. He looked down at it. Four thirty-five! So how much time did he *really* have? And how much of it would he waste, trying to persuade his mom to come out and watch? She'd probably carry on about lateness, and make him put the skateboard away and come in and eat his supper.

So how long? Ten minutes? Fifteen minutes?

Thoughtfully, he skated up the front of his house. Susie was looking at her face in the mirror.

She was always looking at her face in the mirror.

For a while he balanced on the rooftop, breathing the icy air and looking at the stars — they seemed much closer up there. He leaped to a chimney, perching there like a giant crow. Then, punctuating roofs with chimneys and chimneys with roofs, he skated joyfully down the street.

He thought of his school, and in an instant he was on the roof, looking down into the empty playground. It worked! It worked!

Danny jumped into the air.

"I am the champion!" he shouted, beating his chest.

There was no one to hear.

"I can do anything!"

There was no one there to argue. It was too cold. Even Danny was cold. Especially his fingers.

He wondered if he could use his magic to find his gloves. He filled his mind with a picture of them. Red, woolen, and warm. Nice gloves. His grandma had made them for him. He wished himself to be wherever they were.

The skateboard began to move. Down the front of the building it slid and across the playground.

Outside the daycare center it stopped. Now that was wrong — Danny was no baby. He wondered if the magic was already beginning to fade. He listened for the beeps, but his watch was silent.

He tried again, thinking about his lost gloves, even remembering the hole in the thumb.

"Take me," he said, "to my gloves!" It sounded very silly.

And nothing happened at all.

Disappointed, he looked reproachfully down at the skateboard and there, on the ground, lay a single familiar red glove. Just one.

Astonished, he bent down and picked it up. It was frozen — stiff as the hand of a puppet. He was thinking, It won't do me much good, when there was a swoosh and a crackle and a snap, and Danny found himself in complete darkness.

# Chapter Four

Danny should have been frightened.

He was not.

He was curious, though. The place he was in smelled familiar, but he couldn't think why.

He put out his hands like a blind man and his fingers closed around a soft fuzzy object with an odd metal spine. He pulled at the fuzzy thing. It came off in his hand. It was his glove. His other glove.

Danny grinned.

Of course.

He knew where he was.

He felt his way along a row of curved metal spines. He knew what they were.

Just past the place where they ended, he knew there would be a door. He found it. He opened it. Behind the door he knew there would be a light switch. He flipped it on. From the rows of hooks in the school cloakroom, a couple of forgotten gym bags drooped heavily, like over-ripe pears.

Pleased with himself, Danny picked up his skateboard and walked out into the dim hallway. He could just make out the paintings pinned to the wall, and the Christmas decorations. He switched on another light. The polished wooden floor stretched out deliciously in front of him. Skateboarding, he knew, was strictly forbidden inside school.

Down the hall whizzed Danny, down the hall and into the auditorium, flipping light switches along the way. Around the auditorium he skated, round and round and across the stage and over the piano and around again.

He thought of Assembly and giggled — if only his teachers could see him now!

He began to sing a carol, shouting out the words. He knew the words to all of the carols, because he was in the choir. He knew another version of this one. A naughty version, which had nothing to do with Christmas. He sang that one too. He sang it at the top of his voice.

When he stopped, the auditorium was uncomfortably quiet. It was like that awkward silence that happens when nobody knows what to say next.

Danny didn't know what to do next.

He tried transferring himself to his classroom. How strange it looked at night. How dark and empty. He switched on the light and skated across the desk tops. He tried a dozen kick-turns on his teacher's table, and every one of them was perfect. A box of chalk fell to the floor. He stopped and picked it up. The surface of the blackboard had been wiped clean.

Danny looked at it and grinned.

Then he shook out a piece of chalk and began to write:

HAPPY NEW YEAR TO EVERYBODY.

LOVE, DANNY.

He had just gotten to the Y of YEAR when he heard a noise. The sound of a key being turned in a lock. Footsteps. Somebody shouting. It was the custodian.

Danny froze. Now he was in for it. Now there'd be trouble. Breaking and entering — would they call the police? He dropped his chalk, picked up his skateboard, and started to run.

Then he stopped.

Who was a dumb-dumb?

Who was a twit?

He put down his skateboard and stepped on it.

The custodian came running along the hall, a flashlight in his hand. Their eyes met.

"What the . . . ?" the custodian exclaimed.

"Hampstead Heath!" yelled Danny.

# Chapter Five

There was a sound like a small firework exploding, and a rush of icy air, and the custodian's startled eyes and gaping mouth disappeared into a whirling patchwork of black woods and streetlights.

Suddenly Danny found himself standing on the top of a dark hill. Gray grass sloped into shadows and disappeared into dim huddles of trees. Below him, through the frosty air, he could see the city sprinkled across the night like a bowlful of sequins.

Wow! he thought.

He'd been to the Heath before, but never at night. This was breathtaking. He could have stayed up there for hours.

He didn't really know why he'd asked for it—it had just been the first name that had popped into his head:

Hampstead Heath,
Clean your teeth.

He could have asked for home.
He could have wished himself into his best

friend's house.

He just hadn't had time to think.

Now he did.

So the skateboard could travel this far.

How much farther?

The big McDonald's in Piccadilly Circus? But he had no money. A movie, then; he could get in for free. But he wouldn't have time to watch the whole thing. London Airport; he could watch the planes. The seaside? He shivered: too cold. What about France, then, where he'd spent his summer vacation?

What about Africa?

He grinned.

Now he *was* being silly.

Her Time, she'd said. Whatever that was. He looked down at his watch. Four-forty? Did it need a new battery?

Her Time, he thought. Was it special Time?

"You're wasting it . . ."

He whipped around, but there was no one there.

"Think big, Danny!"

He caught a whiff of cinnamon and mothballs.

"Where are you?" he called.

Someone laughed. "You could go a long way, Danny . . ."

He looked up, and there she was, hanging by her boots from the sky, her pale face with its wicked, dark eyes and flowered hat just a few yards above his head.

"Stop gaping, boy, and get on with it."

Danny gasped.

"How do you do that?" he said, but she'd disappeared.

Get on with it.

All right, then. He would.

He took a deep breath.

"Trafalgar Square!"

He skated into the air. The hill he had been standing on fell rapidly backward, and the whole Heath suddenly opened like a fan below him, dark and mysterious. He moved so quickly that the stars above his head turned into a silver scrawl, and all the little cars on the streets below became threads of gold and orange and red.

He began to hear voices. People singing. Water splashing.

A fine spray spattered his cheeks. He was skating around the edge of a fountain. Around and around and around.

Nobody saw him. All the people were looking at an enormous Christmas tree glittering with lights.

Danny jumped down. He picked up his skateboard and wriggled through the crowd, but he was too small to see over people's shoulders. He wondered if he should wish himself closer, but there definitely wasn't any room, even for magic.

People jostled around him in a friendly way, like people at a party. Most of them were singing. A little kid pushed by him, stepping on his toes, yelling for his daddy.

With nothing better to do, Danny joined in the carol, but his eyes were already sliding past the big star on top of the tree, past the fountains and the crouching lions, to something much taller. Something much higher than the Christmas tree. Something with a stone man standing on top, whose hat pointed into the sky.

Danny wondered what kind of a view Admiral Nelson had up there.

Suddenly faces turned into tops of heads. Then heads became blobs, lions became pussycats, and offices, theaters, and government buildings went swooshing into the ground. And the wind whistled past Danny's ears as he skated up and up, to balance breathless at the top, his hand on a cold stone knee.

Only three people saw a boy skateboarding up the side of Nelson's Column.

The first was a poet, who smiled, nibbled the end of his pencil, then wrote in a small blue notebook:

Old warrior
Stone warrior
Put up your sword
For a boy on a skateboard
Is coming aboard.

The second was an old man who carried a sign on a stick. The sign said: BEWARE OF THE WRATH TO COME. When the old man saw Danny, he pointed a quivering finger.

"Behold!" he said. "Angels are already amongst us . . ."

But nobody listened. Nobody ever listened.

The third was a fat five-year-old girl, who tugged at her mother's sleeve.

"Look, Mom! That boy's going up Nelson's Column on a skateboard!"

"Be quiet," said her mom, without turning her head. "You've been watching too much TV."

# Chapter Six

Furious pigeons flapped into the air, their familiar roosts disturbed by a boy who had no business being there at all.

And it was cold. It was so cold that Danny almost forgot to look down.

But beside him, Nelson stared into the night, touched by neither cold nor Christmas, and around them both, the wind howled, and above them both, the stars glittered icily.

Danny shivered. The world below him looked unreal. The Christmas tree he'd wanted to see was just a tinsel toy. The cars were toys, and all the little heads in the crowd were bobbing like flowers in a meadow. Nothing was real, except the wind lashing his cheeks.

A pigeon landed on Danny's head; he could feel the scritch-scratch of its feet in his hair as it marched around. It was heavy, too; he'd never thought a bird could be that heavy. Now he knew how it felt to be a statue. Except that statues didn't feel—not pigeons, not anything. Not even the cold.

Especially not the cold.

Lucky things, thought Danny.

He began to think about warmth. Radiators. Fires. Mugs of hot chocolate. Bowls of soup. Sun. Summer. Beaches . . . He remembered the beach where he'd played during vacation. He remembered the feeling of warm sand running through his fingers, of jumping into the sea to cool down. Summer was like a dream.

A beach like that, he thought, would be great now.

He hadn't meant to make such a very clear picture come into his head. The sand between his toes. The shells. The blue-green water glinting in the sun . . .

That was what he was thinking as he rose into the night.

That was what he was thinking as he watched Trafalgar Square turn into a pattern of lights, a small pattern inside a big one. The big one was London.

The big one became small and vanished. Other patterns took its place. They vanished too. And all the time the stars drew silver threads across an inky sky.

The sky grayed and the threads broke. The sky became primrose and they vanished. Below him lay camouflage country in greens and browns. Below him lay a range of mountains covered in snow. More camouflage country and more mountains. Lakes like shiny coins. Rivers like curly ribbons. Seas. Oceans.

Now he saw a great bridge spanning a harbor.

The skateboard scrunched against sand.

It was hot. It was very hot.

Danny was sweating. He took off his socks and shoes and curled his bare toes in the sand.

The sand was the color of caramel, and people lay all over it, basking in the heat like contented seals. Near him a man and a woman were cuddling. Nobody noticed Danny.

He stood up and looked around. Behind him rose an olive-green lattice of trees. Through it, on a road, he could see cars twinkling. Somewhere, someone began playing a guitar.

Danny wondered where he was. He wondered

where in the world it could be hot and sunny five days before Christmas. Not France, certainly. Africa, perhaps? America? How far had he traveled? How far had he come? He looked at the place where the ocean met the sky.

Which ocean?

He gave up, and watched the waves instead. He watched them growing and curling into breakers. He watched the breakers falling in fountains of white foam. People were surfing in that ocean, their boards skimming the water, light as leaves.

An orange butterfly settled on the back of his hand. He watched it lazily. Surfing, he thought. Must be a little like skateboarding.

He looked at the skateboard lying at his feet.

He looked at his watch. It was only four forty-five.

How much time did he have?

He took off his anorak. He took off his jeans and his sweater and his shirt. He picked up his skateboard and ran to the edge of the ocean. Foam creamed around his toes, and his feet sank two hollows into the wet sand.

He put the skateboard down and stepped on
it.

Somebody laughed.

Somebody shouted, "You can't surf on that
thing!"

He could, of course.

And he did.

No problem.

For Danny rode the waves like a small sea
god, sliding up the curved green walls of water
and gliding along inside them. The tops of the

waves, where they broke and met the sky, were
full of dancing lights. The depths were like old
bottles—lustrous greens and smoky browns and
amber, like his mom's earrings. Never in his life
had he seen anything so marvelous. He could
have gone on doing this forever.

Almost weeping, he forced himself to turn
back to the beach. How much time had he used
up now?

And how would he get home if all the magic
ran out?

As he waded out of the water a boy came up to him.

"You can't surf on one of those things," he said.

"Well, I just did," said Danny.

"I know," said the boy admiringly. "What's the trick?"

Danny shrugged.

"It's easy, really," he said modestly. "Nothing to it, if you know how."

He walked up the beach feeling rather superior.

The other boy tagged along behind.

"Show me," he was saying. "Will you? Will you show me?"

Danny struggled into his clothes, grateful that his underpants had dried so quickly in the hot sun. He was beginning to worry. How much time was left? Would she warn him?

Perhaps he should go home right now.

Then he thought of something really ridiculous.

Really silly.

Mischievous.

He grinned.

For he had a cousin. And his cousin lived in France.

He would stop off and visit him. On his way home. From wherever he was. Wish him a Merry Christmas. Give him a shock.

He thought about his cousin's house. His room.

The other boy was saying, "Why do you need an anorak in the middle of December?"

But the rest of his words were lost.

# Chapter Seven

The ocean fell away.

Then it was gone, swallowed by the olive and gold of the land.

Mountains.

Valleys.

He was flying backward into dawn. The sky paled, blushed, then burned with orange fire. It yellowed, turned lime, blued, turned violet, grayed, and deepened into night. Stars silvered the night sky. The moon rolled around like an ivory ball. Cities twinkled and vanished. Clouds grew, spread, and blackened, and lightning streaked across them. Then they shrank and disappeared. Thunder crashed, growled, and faded into a thin whine. It rained, then stopped. Danny put out his tongue and caught a snowflake.

Then he was in his cousin's room, sitting on the floor.

Matthew was lying on the bed, reading a comic book.

"Hi, Matt," said Danny, shaking raindrops out of his hair.

Matthew looked angry.

"You splashed me," he said.

Then he sat up very straight and his eyes grew large.

"You're supposed to be in England."

"That's right," agreed Danny cheerfully. "I just came over to wish you a Merry Christmas!"

He suddenly panicked.

"I've got to pee," he yelled. "See you."

On the way to the bathroom he thought boastfully, I could pee anywhere. In the Eiffel Tower. In a Hovercraft. In Buckingham Palace, even.

Well, why not?

His aunt's bathroom was ordinary.

His aunt's bathroom was like everyone else's bathroom.

He took a deep breath.

"The Queen's bathroom, Buckingham Palace."

Nothing to it, he thought. Just like asking for half fare to Tottenham.

The hallway swirled.

He added hastily, "If she's not using it."

He heard Matthew shouting, "Hey, you can't just turn up like that —"

Then there was the familiar crackle as Danny snapped through the ceiling and out into the night.

# Chapter Eight

A city sparkled below him.

Was it Paris? wondered Danny.

But as he tried to pick out the Eiffel Tower, the sparkle winked out.

Darkness.

Then he saw the glitter of another city.

The glitter split into lines of streetlights as Danny skateboarded high above the river and sailed across the bright clock face of Big Ben.

London. His town.

He checked on the time. The huge metal

hands were pointing to a ten and a five: four-fifty. Danny looked at his watch. The pattern hadn't changed. Her Time, he thought. Silly Time. Hardly moved. Hardly changed. Had she stuck all the clocks with Super Glue?

He flew over Piccadilly Circus, skimming the dazzle of the big Coca-Cola sign and the curve of colored stars above Regent Street. Pigeons swerved and scattered as he looped back to Trafalgar Square, swooped down past Nelson, made rings around the Christmas tree, and slid up and over the big stone arch. He could see cars moving slowly up and down The Mall. He could see the tangle of trees in St. James's Park.

He skated over the head of Queen Victoria. He skated over the wrought iron gates of the Palace. The sentries in their boxes scanned the courtyard and the street, but they didn't look up. Why should they? They were trained to deal with people on the ground, not a boy on a flying skateboard.

And snap! Danny was through the walls.

Snap! Snap! Snap! (The Palace has lots of rooms.)

Snap!
Snap!
Snap!

Snap! Snap! Snap!

He came to rest in complete darkness.

There was a faint smell of perfume. Hers? he wondered.

He stretched out his hands and found a wall. Its surface was slippery, like silk.

His fingers slid along it in search of a switch. They curled around a thing like a carved flower. They touched the middle, and the room lit up.

Danny jumped back, blinking.

Most of the light came from a chandelier. A splendid chandelier, all diamonds and rainbows. He'd seen one in a movie, but this was real, and for a second he stood there, gaping.

And above it, on the ceiling, plaster cherubs with garlands of golden flowers were dancing in a ring.

Wow! thought Danny.

This was it.

So who wanted ordinary ceilings?

And who on earth wanted dumb old lamps? Boring. Boring.

When he grew up, he was going to have gold stuff on his ceiling. And a chandelier in his bathroom.

He was going to have chandeliers all over his house.

He looked down and suddenly saw his scuffed, laced-up boots and the turned-up ends of his jeans framed in a carpet of rich crimson. And across that carpet, two lines of gold thread made a pathway to a seat of rose-flecked marble. The seat was supported by two carved lions, and at its back lay a cushion of purple velvet, with heavy gold tassels at each corner.

And above the seat hung a canopy, with roses and thistles and shamrocks and leeks entwined around its edges, and above that, there was a statue of a lady in a long nightgown, wearing a helmet and carrying a big fork.

Danny snorted.

He thought she looked stupid.

So what? He had something important to do.

He walked boldly up to the seat.

He lifted the lid. The seat was padded with ermine. Politely, he lifted the seat, his fingers caressing the fur.

Across the back of the bowl the words *By Appointment* were written in curly letters. Well, I've made one, he thought. By wishing.

He tugged at his zipper.

Inside the bowl, the water was pale turquoise and it smelled of flowers.

Danny was ready.

The turquoise greened.

When he finished, he reached up. In the gold handle of the chain a single ruby was glowing crimson, like that special lipstick his mom sometimes wore.

He pulled.

There should have been music or something, he thought, not that boring old *whoosh* you could have heard anywhere. A roll of drums. Trumpets, at least.

He looked down.

The water was turquoise again.

Danny felt pleased with himself. Impressed. Well, who else would have thought of peeing in the Queen's toilet?

This would change everything.

He would make them all respect him now, he thought. The bully who punched him when no one was looking. The skateboard show-off who sneered, "Look at Danny the wonder boy! Look at him wobbling!"

And his kid brother, who pestered him.

And his big sister—what had she ever done? Apart from looking at her face in the mirror.

From this moment on, Danny was special.

He turned to look at the room. He wanted to remember every detail. Not that he could tell anybody. Not that anyone would believe him if he did.

He touched a roll of toilet paper held in the paws of a small jade griffin. It was gossamer-soft and each sheet was printed with the royal coat of arms.

He carefully removed a single sheet, folded it, and put it in his pocket.

On the far wall hung a marble sink shaped like a scallop shell and inlaid with little golden fish. When Danny filled it with water, the fish seemed to swim.

On both sides of the sink stood two little bars of soap—one a lion, the other a unicorn. He washed his hands with the lion and dried them on a crimson towel initialed with the letters *E II R*.

How he longed to tell someone.

Suddenly he saw his reflection in the huge gilt mirror, and for an instant, he was more amazed at the sight of his own familiar face—a little sandy, a little sweaty—than anything else.

Near the mirror, he spotted a lipstick case. He pulled off the top and wound up the stick. It was just like a crayon—a red wax crayon with a nicely sharpened point.

# Chapter Nine

"Time, Danny!"

Danny whipped around guiltily. Where was she? Some of the lipstick had stuck to his fingers.

The voice came from everywhere and nowhere.

"Time, Danny!"

"Time, Danny . . ."

"Time, Danny . . ."

There was a smell of cinnamon and mothballs.

And his watch was beeping wildly.

The skateboard came rolling across the carpet.

He stepped on it, and the room exploded.

The chandelier sparkled and spun like a pinwheel.

Snap! And Danny was through the wall.

Crack! Snap! And ambassadors and suits of armor, portraits and porcelain, footmen and flowers, butlers and cooks, ladies-in-waiting and Welsh corgis and kennel maids all went flying around his head.

Crack! Snap! And he was out, skating over London, and the sky was full of giant dandelion heads of silver and fuchsia and gold.

The dandelion heads all burst into clocks.

"Puff! Twelve o'clock. Puff! One o'clock."
Someone was telling the time. "Puff! Two
o'clock. Puff! Three. Four-thirty. Four-forty.
Four forty-five. Four-fifty. Four fifty-five and
stop, stop, stop!"

He was trying to catch some of the drifting seeds when a black straw hat appeared beneath him.

Danny slid into its comforting interior. Had it grown? he wondered.

Or had she shrunk him? He was still trying to make up his mind as the hat sailed down, gentle as a shadow, black as night, and tipped him out on his own doorstep. Then it rose and floated, like a big balloon, up and over the rooftops.

The beep turned itself off. Five o'clock.

Her Time, thought Danny. Silly time. Crazy time.

He checked himself quickly. No, he hadn't shrunk.

He looked at his skateboard. It seemed the same, but it felt different. Heavier. Earthbound.

He put it down. The rollers rattled along the sloping path, and the curved end went crashing against the gate. Reluctantly, he went over and picked it up. She'd fixed it, he thought sadly. And now she'd unfixed it. No more flying, and he'd liked flying. And no more chandeliers; just Susie's tights dripping into the bathtub, and his brother's wind-up dolphin lying on its side.

And yet . . .

It was still his skateboard. Even without the magic. It was the nice birthday skateboard his dad had given him.

He swung open the gate and scooted down to the nearest streetlight. Dreamily he balanced, rocked, then, without thinking, flipped into a perfect turn.

Wow! he thought.

He tried another.

"I can do it!" he yelled. "I don't need her old magic," and to prove it, he did it again.

Cool, thought Danny.

He ran back to the house and banged at the front door.

"Come and watch!"

His sister opened it. When she saw him, she yawned.

"It's only Danny," she called out. She'd put on big clip-on earrings and a silly pink bow. He thought she looked stupid.

They were all in the back room watching TV.

One of the cats was asleep on the radiator.

His mom looked up at him.

"You're late," she said. "Weren't you cold out there?"

Danny dumped his skateboard and sat down. Fuss, fuss, fuss. She was always fussing. Anyone would think he was a little kid.

And what was there to say? She wouldn't believe him. Nobody would believe him. He wasn't even sure he believed it himself.

He put his hands in his pockets. In one of them he found a carefully folded piece of incredibly soft toilet paper.

He took it out and opened it.

He looked at it.

Secretly.

"Just listen to this," said his mom.

The newscaster was saying, "A violation of the Queen's private rooms in Buckingham Palace is now thought to be nothing more serious than a prank, possibly perpetrated by a very junior member of the Queen's household. However, police are investigating."

And there appeared on the screen a large mirror with a gold frame, and across its surface were crayoned the words:

Danny
was here

Susie smirked and pointed.

"Oh, yes," she said. "So that's where you've been."

Danny put the piece of paper back in his pocket and grinned.

"As a matter of fact," he said, "it was."

He glanced out the window into the dark night.

A small, thin shape was sailing across the stars.

It might, he supposed, have been an airplane.

But then, it might not.